This igloo book belongs to:

....

igloobooks

Published in 2016
by Igloo Books Ltd
Cottage Farm
Sywell
NN6 0BJ
www.igloobooks.com

LEO002 0116
2 4 6 8 10 9 7 5 3 1
ISBN 978-1-78557-650-8

Written by Sienna Williams
Illustrated by Kate Daubney

Printed and manufactured in China

Magnificent Millie

by Sienna Williams

illustrated by
Kate Daubney

igloobooks

Millie Mouse loved **inventing things** more than mice love cheese! She wanted to help her woodland friends with her ideas, but things didn't always go to plan.

Mole couldn't see anything through the **super specs.**

Rabbit's **Bounce Booster** flung her over the treetops.

Woodpecker got a **headache** from the **Pecking Protector.**

Frog's ***Tongue Tonic*** made his tongue too sticky!

Tongue Tonic

One sunny morning, the animals decided to have a picnic.
"I've got lots of ideas to help us get ready!" cried Millie, excitedly.
As usual, things soon began to go wrong.

The **TURNIP EXTRACTOR** sent Badger's turnips zooming into the sky.

Then there was Squirrel's **Super-Sucker...** ... It shot acorns all over the place!

The **BALLOON BLOWER** made Hedgehog huff and puff until he was completely out of breath.

Everyone had just about had enough, when...

... Millie tried to lay out the picnic blankets with her

splendid spinner.

As Millie pedalled, the machine whirred and clicked, faster and **faster**, until...

...WHOOOOSH!

Millie's invention flung the picnic blankets everywhere and the animals were **very cross**.

"Maybe it's time for me to **stop** inventing once and for all," said Millie. "My ideas only seem to cause **trouble.**"

With that, Millie scurried away into the woods.

Suddenly, Millie came across a giant picnic basket. "It must have fallen out of that delivery van," she said, as the van disappeared into the distance.

The enormous picnic basket was full of delicious treats. "It's too big to carry all the way home," said Millie. "If I invent something to bring it back, I'm sure everyone will forgive me."

When Millie showed her friends and explained her plan, they
shook their heads. "We'll bring it back ourselves," said Tortoise.
"We can't have another of your inventions going wrong."

Millie's friends tried everything they could think of to get the feast home.

They heaved...

... and strained, but it wasn't long before they were all ready to give up.

"It looks like we do need your help after all," they told Millie.
Millie was delighted. "I've got the perfect idea," she said.

"Best of all, we can build it **together!**"

The animals busied themselves
gathering things to build the invention.
Soon they were ready to begin.

TOOLS

They lifted...

... they hammered...

.... they sawed and bolted.

Finally, the invention was finished.

Everyone gasped when they saw what they had created.
"Allow me to demonstrate," announced Millie ...

"The ... Fantabulous Food-Flinger!"

Millie jumped on with a...

... "One,
two,
three!"

BOING... SWOOSH!

The food went soaring over the treetops and everyone clapped and cheered.

Soon, everyone wanted to try the Fantabulous Food-Flinger for themselves...

... so, one by one, the animals each sent a piece of the picnic flying into the distance.

Sure enough, when they arrived at Poppy Meadow, the picnic was ready and waiting for them.

"We did it!" they cried.

Everyone munched and chomped on the delicious picnic feast all afternoon.
"You really are a **magnificent** inventor, Millie," said Rabbit.
The others nodded in agreement.

"I couldn't have done any of it without my **magnificent** friends,"
said Millie, as she polished off the very last bite of cheese.
"Working together made the best invention **ever!**"